Rooster Can't Cock-a-Doodle-Doo

by **Karen Rostoker-Gruber**
pictures by **Paul Rátz de Tagyos**

DIAL BOOKS FOR YOUNG READER NEW YORK

Many thanks to the Bound Book Writers, Wendy Pfeffer, Ann Porzio Lewis, and Karen Riskin for making this book the best it could be—K.R.G.

Published by Dial Books for Young Readers
A division of Penguin Young Readers Group
345 Hudson Street
New York, New York 10014
Text copyright © 2004 by KRG Entertainment, LLC
Pictures copyright © 2004 by Paul Rátz de Tagyos
All rights reserved
Designed by Kimi Weart
Text set in Novarese
Manufactured in China on acid-free paper

10 9 8 7 6 5 4 3 2

Library of Congress Cataloging-in-Publication Data
Rostoker-Gruber, Karen.
Rooster can't cock-a-doodle-doo / by Karen Rostoker-Gruber;
pictures by Paul Rátz de Tagyos.
p. cm.
Summary: When Rooster's throat is too sore for him to crow,
the other farm animals help both him and Farmer Ted.
ISBN 0-8037-2877-8
|1. Roosters—Fiction. 2. Domestic animals—Fiction. 3. Farm life—Fiction.
4. Sick—Fiction.| I. Rátz de Tagyos, Paul, ill. II. Title.
PZ7.R72375 Ro 2004
|E|—dc21
2002014625

The drawings were penciled, inked, and then colored with markers on marker paper.
 A teeny-weeny bit of color pencil was sometimes used (but that's cheating).—P.R.d.T.

One morning, Rooster woke up with a terrible sore throat.

"Oh, no!" he coughed. "What should I do?
My throat hurts too much to cock-a-doodle-doo!"
Rooster wondered how he was going to wake up Farmer Ted
and the animals without cock-a-doodle-dooing.

He went to the hen house.
No one was collecting eggs.
The hens were asleep.

COUGH! COUGH!

"Wake up, Hens," Rooster whispered.

"I can't cock-a-doodle-doo!"

"You poor thing. You look *eggz-hausted*," clucked the hens.

"How will you wake up Farmer Ted without cock-a-doodle-dooing?"

"Maybe the cows will know," said Rooster.

The hens followed Rooster
to the cow barn.

No one was getting milked.
The cows were asleep.

COUGH! COUGH!

CLUCK! CLUCK!

"Wake up, Cows," they said. "Rooster can't cock-a-doodle-doo!"

"Oh, my! How *udder-ly* frustrating," mooed the cows.

"How will you wake up Farmer Ted without cock-a-doodle-dooing?"

"Maybe the sheep will know," said Rooster.

The hens and cows followed Rooster to the sheep pasture.

No one was getting sheared.

The sheep were asleep.

COUGH! COUGH!

CLUCK! CLUCK!

MOO! MOO!

"Wake up, Sheep," they said. "Rooster can't cock-a-doodle-doo!"

"That's *baaad baaad* news!" baaed the sheep. "How will you wake up Farmer Ted without cock-a-doodle-dooing?"

"Maybe the pigs will know," said Rooster.

The hens, cows, and sheep
followed Rooster to the pigpen.
No one was pouring slop.
The pigs were asleep.

COUGH! COUGH!

CLUCK! CLUCK!

MOO! MOO!

BAA! BAA!

"Wake up, Pigs," they said. "Rooster can't cock-a-doodle-doo!"

"Oh, dear! That's a *muddy* big problem!" oinked the pigs.

"How will you wake up Farmer Ted without cock-a-doodle-dooing?"

"You don't know?" baaed the sheep. "Now what will we do?
There's no one left to ask!"

"Let's go to Farmer Ted's house," Rooster said.

"We'll just walk right in and wake him up."

The hens, cows, sheep, and pigs
followed Rooster to Farmer Ted's house.

THE HOUSE WAS LOCKED.

"Oh, my! Now no one will ever collect our eggs," clucked the hens.

"If someone doesn't milk us, we're going to burst!" mooed the cows.

"Our wool is so long, we're tripping on it," baaed the sheep.

"We're starving!" oinked the pigs.

Rooster felt awful. This was all his fault.

Farmer Ted's bedroom was on the third floor,

and there was no way to wake him.

UNLESS . . .

"I've got it," Rooster whispered. The animals huddled around him.

Then . . .

The sheep stood on the cows.

The pigs stood on the sheep.

The hens stood on the pigs.

And Rooster stood on top.

"Will you please *moo-ve* your hooves?

They're right in our eyes," mooed the cows.

"We would, if our friends the swine would stop

wiggling their tails in our faces," baaed the sheep.

"Well, tell the feather-brained quartet

to quit tickling our snouts," oinked the pigs.

"Who are you calling the feather-brained quartet?"

clucked the hens.

"Oh, my! What's all this ruckus?" said Farmer Ted
as he opened his window.
COUGH! COUGH! Rooster pointed to his sore throat.

Farmer Ted squinted at the sun. "It's getting late," he said,
putting on his overalls.
"I have to finish the chores before the sun sets,
or I won't be able to see what I'm doing."

He warmed up some tea with honey for Rooster
and carried him to a chair by the pond.
Then he quickly set out to work.

The animals watched Farmer Ted.

"He's never going to finish the chores before sunset,"
clucked the hens.

"Pr*obaaably* not," baaed the sheep.

"We've got to help him before our milk curdles,"
mooed the cows.

"We have an idea," oinked the pigs.

The animals huddled together.

Then . . .

They helped Farmer Ted collect the eggs,

milk the cows,

shear the sheep,

and pour the slop.

The sun set. After their busy day, the animals
and Farmer Ted were ready for bed.
Rooster had rested all day on the chair by Farmer
Ted's pond. His throat was nice and warm from the
tea he'd sipped, and his feet even had a slight tan.
He felt much better.

"Thanks for your help today."

Cock-a-doodle-doo!

he crowed with all his might.

"Glad to help—just please pipe down," clucked the hens.

"We're trying to get some sleep," mooed the cows.

"Give it a rest," baaed the sheep.

"Save it for the morning," oinked the pigs.

And that's exactly what Rooster did.